Beer-Breath Kisses

Damon McKinney

Fort Smith, Arkansas

BEER-BREATH KISSES

Cover image © Steve Snodgrass
via Wikimedia Commons,
under the Creative Commons Attribution 2.0 Generic license
Author photograph © Sara McKinney

Edited by Casie Dodd
Design & typography by Belle Point Press

Belle Point Press
Fort Smith, Arkansas
bellepointpress.com
editor@bellepointpress.com

Find Belle Point Press
on Facebook,
Twitter (@BellePointPress),
and Instagram (@bellepointpress)

Printed in the United States of America

27 26 25 24 23   1 2 3 4 5

ISBN: 978-1-960215-02-4

CHAP6/BPP13

CONTENTS

OSHKASHÎWIWA

I hear coyotes yapping in the distance, singing their song to the moon mother. My heart yearns to learn their song, but my voice can't match the notes or rhythm. The only noise I make is a low hum-growl, throaty and guttural. Primal. They don't hear me and keep yapping, singing, and dancing on the Oklahoma red earth. Car lights flash in the distance and the singing stops. Back to work.

I'm awake now, the sun leaning heavily on us 'skins working the road crew. Paving highway roads, patchin' potholes, and getting yelled at for trying to earn a legal living. We get paid $15 an hour to hold a Slow Down sign and yet we're called drunks, crackheads, and lazy freeloaders. Most people think it's court-ordered community service, but it ain't. Just regular work for the county. I make more money selling dope, except that business doesn't offer insurance. The county does.

Once, I heard a wolf howling.

t was a humid, stifling, sweltering summer day. Hot enough to drive a man crazy. In my dad's case, pack up all his shit and drive off. I watched that truck rumble down the dirt road as sweat and tears trickled down my face. It was the heat that made him leave and not the baggage they hauled from one Montana reservation to Maryland and finally to an even poorer reservation in Oklahoma. It was the heat—miserable, unending, and drama-inducing heat. I like to think that, but maybe it was looking at me and seeing another man's face. It wasn't my fault. It was the heat.

CORNER POCKET

The tables were never level and the felt hadn't been replaced in quite some time, but they were what you learned on. They were slick and smooth, causing the balls to run just a little further. You adjusted your shots accordingly and often. The rails were fast and loose; they added to the bounce of your shots. The sticks were mostly straight. The cue ball was chipped and the eight was a solid black ball someone painted the "8" on. Cigarette smoke as thick as snow drifts on the Flathead, which you'd never see again, and the beer was cold, and everyone was desperate. This was your home, born and raised. You ran those tables ever since you were old enough to ask your mom for fifty cents.

Beer-Breath Kisses

Along with the usual problems—having water or lights, having enough food or medicine for the babies—there were also the "white people" problems. Religion, politics, social structure, runaway fathers, dead uncles, miscarriages, abortions, and why Momma killed Joel's puppy—truth is she didn't see the little bastard until he was squished. We, my cousins and I, never talked about dead grandparents, hurt feelings, or what to do about grief; we plowed through our lives. We bullied and pushed aside anyone who tried to love us.

The old man fought in the WWII, won a few chest goodies, and loved more than a few women along the way. He kept it all locked away in his wooden footlocker, tucked under his bed, including the shell shock. He'd make his kids—five girls and a rowdy boy—keep fire watch and patrol around the neighborhood at night. Maybe that's what hardened them against the world. The old woman, Grandma, wasn't great by any means. She had a quick temper and an even meaner bite. Forced assimilation at a residential school, she took more than her share of beatings for speaking her native tongue, being prideful, and not being born white. She passed that simmering anger—rage really—on her kids. The old man bought their home on the G.I. Bill, but it wasn't worth all the blood and horror. Grandma didn't care for anyone after a few drinks, nor could she keep her peace: "Why you cryin', boy? He ain't even your *real* daddy," she'd say. The old man nodded with secret knowledge. "That bastard ran off and never looked back," she followed, swallowing another beer. "But I love you, sonny."

Our mothers and uncle were fighters. They fought boyfriends, girlfriends, the law, and each other. Knockdown drag-out fights in the front yard, beer bottles thrown across the bar, and missing baby doll heads, secreted away in a closet. After every fight, they'd make up and keep on going. Until the next time. We would go weeks without seeing each other because our moms were fighting. Once, we watched our aunt beat the shit out of her best friend over a man. It was a Sunday afternoon, and everyone was at the bar, hanging out, drinking—soda for us kids—and having a good time. We heard the heavy steel door slam shut and the unmistakable sound of flip flops slapping on the concrete floor. There was yelling and shouting, and we could see our aunt in the thick of it, reaching for her best friend by the hair and jerking her off her barstool. Her legs flew over her head and our aunt was on her, punching and slapping her face. Our aunt stood up and kicked her—still wearing flip flops—once, twice, three times in the face. By this time, my mother and the other sisters joined my aunt, yelling and swearing, shouting "lululululu" while the other woman bled on the concrete floor. The old man and Grandma kept on drinking.

Our mothers said they loved us. At times it was hard to tell with the yelling, spankings with Hot Wheel tracks, and being locked out of the house. They showed their love by working dead-end jobs, staying late, and making miracles for Christmas. They supported us in our school activities—band, choir, or whatever we'd join to escape.

But sometimes, their own habits got in the way. My mom missed a band performance because she had to make a drug run to Cleveland. She figured she would have time, but she didn't make it back to see me perform. I was standing outside the concert hall, trombone in hand, when they finally showed up. Her idea to make me forgive her was to let me rent a movie and eat pizza. It still hurts. The next morning, she even made breakfast.

The sisters were all business during the week, but the weekends were something else. Friday nights they could be found at the Wayside Inn, the bar our grandparents owned, drinking, dancing, shooting pool, and having a grand old time. We were left at home to fend for ourselves; luckily the local movie theater cost 99 cents to see a semi-current movie. We must have seen *Jerry Maguire* a dozen times. They'd come home—usually with a guy—all sloppy, happy, drunk. Give us beer-breath kisses and vanish to their bedrooms. We would find quarters and stolen pool chalk on the kitchen tables in the morning, the guys gone. Saturdays were no different, except maybe a different guy.

Sundays were for family dinners. We gathered at the old man's place for supper—usually fried chicken, baked hams, or spaghetti with meatballs. There wasn't enough room for everyone to sit at the table, so we kids sat in the living room. We didn't mind the fleas too much, presents from the neighborhood dogs that came and went. The old man loved those dogs, slamming the screen door all day long, and he wouldn't stop them coming. Grandpa sat at the head of the table and Grandma on his right. The sisters would crowd around the little table, with one standing by the stove dishing out food to the others. Sweet tea, water, pop, and milk. Everything was passed to the left and one of us kids would say, "Thank you, Lord, for this food and bless everyone here. Amen." Forks scraping on ceramic plates, ice clanking around colored metal cups, and an occasional burp. In the summer, we grilled hot dogs and chicken legs. The grass was cut, and the air smelled of summer rain in the distance. We had an old picnic table and a smaller table made from pieces of plywood, kind of like a jigsaw puzzle. One of Grandma's brothers made it before he died. Rust-colored and hardly sanded, it was prickly and a bit of a pain in the ass. But that's where we sat.

After dinner, summer or winter, everyone piled into a car and headed to the bar. Didn't really matter which one—there was always one open on Sunday. We kids rode in the back of a pickup, before seatbelt laws, and bounced around on the red dirt roads. By the time we reached the bar, we were covered in red dust and plastered in sweat. RC Cola and cheap pizzas hit the spot. We'd bother our moms for quarters, which the pool tables and jukebox took. They'd finally get tired of us begging and would give us money to leave them alone. The family sat at the very back of the bar, watching the front and back doors, by the restrooms. They always smelled like piss, the restrooms. There was a stage back there too, but no band ever played. That's what the jukebox was for.

Growing up, there were only three places we could go during the summer: the creek behind Grandpa's house, the swimming pool, or to the Wayside. Given that the bar was an option showed how limited our

7

choices really were. The creek was home to crawdads, which we would use as bait. We'd get one of Grandma's strainers and go scoop those mud bugs out of the creek and into one of Grandpa's stolen buckets. Not that he'd notice it missing, but if he did find it in our grimy little hands, there'd be hell to pay. Often, we were told to "stay outta my stuff, y'all gonna break sumthin' that I can't get any more." It's just that all the cool stuff was his, and we coveted all of it. When we went to the creek, we'd spend all day down there, splashing around and trying to stay cool in the hundred-degree heat of central Oklahoma. Creek County. Drumright to be exact, the heart of Tornado Alley, and home of the biggest oil bust the country had ever seen. More than once, Mom pointed out the exact spot on Main Street where my uncle kicked the shit out of five cops. She spoke with pride about it. That's the legacy we were kin to and expected to carry on. Small towns in Oklahoma don't know they're dead; even today, you can see old pump jacks sucking up something of their former glory. But it just ain't happening.

You once told me, "Most guys will call you a motherfucker all night long. Talking shit. They really don't want to fight. But the moment one puts their hands on you, knock them the fuck out and don't stop."

The phone rang incessantly, jolting Jack back to reality. Visions of vacations and promotions fluttered away—feathers into the ether. Who could be calling? The Monday meeting hadn't been announced. Jack looked past the phone and watched the snowdrift against his office window. Case files cluttered his IKEA desk—all the known knowledge of his charges—and the ringing phone. Empty Red Bull cans dotted the floor near the trash can as well as crimpled wrappers of protein bars. Time to let the cleaning crew in. Again, the phone demanded his attention. Jack snatched the phone off the cradle: "Jack here."

His heels clicked on the linoleum as Jack made his way to the operations office. He hated this part of his job. Haven't they been through enough? Jack reached the office and assessed the scene. The staff—in full-on panic mode—looked up at him and started talking all at once. Jack took over and issued orders. He'd done this before.

"Call the sheriff and the medical examiner. Lock down the boys in their dorms, and don't give any information out, don't answer questions, and keep them busy. I want a head count before breakfast. Is that clear? Call all counselors in, and I don't care if it's their day off."

He swigged down the last of his Red Bull. "Take me there."

"I knew something was wrong when the door wouldn't open. It felt heavy, like something was blocking it," Sam told Jack as they made their way across the campus. "I pushed until it budged a little, and that's when I saw the gray sweatpants." Sam, the janitor, haggard and worn out. Too many late nights cleaning vomit and shit as the boys detoxed. "Brace yourself," Jack whispered, mostly to himself.

"Huh? Say something?" Sam asked.

"No."

"I finally got the door open, and I knew I was too late," Sam continued. "I know I shouldn't have touched him, but I couldn't leave him like that. I got a boy about the same age and it didn't seem right, I don't know."

"You did good, Sam. I'll take it from here. Take the rest of the day off, if you need," Jack offered.

The body was cold. This was the third suicide in the janitor's closet, and Jack knew the other boys would be drawn there. Their morbid curiosity drove them to that quiet mecca, their private place to commune with Death. Jack had tried, unsuccessfully, to get it locked at night, but the proctors argued it needed to be left open in case of new intakes during the late hours. Even after the room was cleaned, the boys loitered around in search of a sign—a scrawled word in Sharpie or a bit of his clothing.

Something.

Jack looked at Death, the boy's face twisted in a peaceful grimace—blue-faced with glassy eyes staring into the void. There was no beauty here.

Sam wiped his eyes. "I got a boy."

After the medical examiner removed the body, after the sheriff cleared the scene, and after he set everything back to "normal," Jack returned to his meager office. The trash was still piled up and someone left a Red Bull on his desk. Only then did he start to sob, slowly at first. His body shook and he rocked back and forth, arms wrapped tightly around himself, as he quietly cried. Tears streamed down his cheeks as he tried to fight his emotions. He heaved and trembled, sighed and wailed his frustration. He took a deep breath and forced himself calm. "Brace yourself."

He packed his belongings into a mover's box. Gathered up the trash on the floor and threw it away. No more daydreams about vacations or promotions. The snow continued to blow against the window, and as he shut the door, the phone began to ring again.

From Delray to Daddy

I t was in the wintertime. I was cold and frightened. And then, I felt his hands. He had worked so hard, for so long, yet they were gentler than any man's. He touched his own children in this same way: five girls and a rowdy boy. The way he touched me let me know that I had brought him that same joy.

It was springtime. I was anxious and on the run. And then, he called my name. Usually it was Joey or Joseph. But my task was always the same. Those dirty, greasy, gentle hands were too big, and that nut or bolt was just beyond their reach. It was in this need that Sonny had the chance to learn, and Daddy had the chance to teach.

It was summertime. It was in the cool, murky water of Lake Allen that I overcame my fear and affirmed that I trusted him. I also learned how to bait a hook, to clean a gun, to respect everything, large or small. They never saw a failure, those soft patient eyes; my daddy saw the promise of his labor.

It is early autumn now. I'm cold and frightened because I feel it won't be long. I can hear the drums. I can smell the smoke. I can hear the bitter harmony of that almost-forgotten farewell song. I will see those patient eyes closed to sleep. I will reach out to hold those gentle hands; those dirty, greasy, just-out-of-reach . . . the ones that mean more to me than any other man's.

sjm

JACK DANIELS AND A PORCH SWING

The wind whistled outside the silver trailer, strong enough to gently rock it back and forth. Philip heard the leaves crinkle and crackle on their limbs and the telltale sound of rain falling on the roof. He pulled himself up off the couch and lurched toward the kitchenette, slightly drunk, and rummaged through the cabinets for pots. Those holes aren't going to fix themselves. He never seemed to have enough pots and usually gave up—*screw it, it'll dry out, always does*—only to stumble back to his couch. And the bottle of Jack Daniels.

He took another deep pull off the bottle and felt that old familiar burn, running down his throat and killing more than a few brain cells as well as washing away pain. He sat there, watching his red-and-white TV—the color tube burned out—and wiped away a single tear. Time for another drink. More burn and fewer memories. Outside the wind calmed down and the rain still splattered against the metal roof.

Those raindrops thundered down.

The roads were slick with water and oil, but his mother drove steely-nerved and white-knuckled the whole way. Those miles passed without a word between them. His mom was the one who took the phone call that prompted the mad dash. His brother on the other end was a panicked mess; Philip could tell it in the way their mother answered his questions. "What? Slow down. Did you call 911? Okay, they're on the way. Okay, we're on our way." Philip jerked on a hoodie and chased after his mom.

It was ten miles. It felt more like one. As they approached the house, Philip saw red-and-white strobe lights, flashing against the lightning. The ambulance blocked the driveway, and they were forced to park on the street. The wind violently blew the wooden porch swing against the single-pane bedroom window. Philip rode that swing a time or two growing up and always got yelled at for banging into the same window. That old porch swing held on for all its worth—between grandkids and stormy nights—and never cracked that window.

Philip followed his mom into the house. Two paramedics worked on the old man lying in the middle of the living room floor. The old man: Grandpa, Daddy, Wilson. He raised five beautiful girls and one rowdy boy in that house. The paramedics, boys really, worked as a team, fighting death and losing—pumping on his chest and ventilating him wasn't going well. One continued CPR while the second prepped the defibrillator. Jack, Philip's brother, sat in the corner.

Jack tried to smoke a cigarette with trembling hands while looking stoic, but he failed at both. His bloodshot brown eyes betrayed his feelings as anguish rolled down his cheeks. The old man wore pajama pants and a plain white T-shirt. He was missing a slipper; its mate lay in the bedroom. Violently peaceful. The paramedics attacked his body, but he didn't have a care in the world.

"You can stop," Jack announced as he stirred from his thoughts. The finality in his words echoed throughout the old home. The medics paused and then renewed their efforts. The defibrillator, anxious to prove its worth, hummed softly. A medic grabbed the handles and rubbed them together.

"Please," Jack begged.

Philip came to on the floor. The bottle of whiskey had tipped over and the brown painkiller leaked out. The red-and-white TV belted out the national anthem, then static. He threw away the empty and fished around in his cabinets for another. His trembling hand clutched a bottle, and he stumbled out the front door. The air smelled clean and fresh—new and forgiving. The sky sparkled, and the moon hung high and silver. He sat on the old porch swing and took a long swig—resuming the cycle.

NORTH CULBERHOUSE

The worst part is going back. Digging through the mire, mud, and muck of memories to find that one clean image. That's why I smoked dope in the first place—to forget. Dirty hands for dirty jobs. And those few good ones, without *him*, stretch—blackhole-gravity-light-destroying—beyond what I can enjoy. I am a child again, running home to seek out forgiveness, closure, and finally, peace.

The *swish, swish, swish* of a cornstalk broom woke me up. I was a heavy sleeper, but that gentle sound startled me. Again, it rang out. *Swish, swish, swish,* 3 a.m. *He's* out in the garage. Sweeping the concrete. What did she do this time? *His* go-to ritual for calming down. I hated it. Maybe that's why now I do it too.

Through the door, I heard *him* mumbling, a murmur, a scant sound of voicing anger. *Swish, swish, swish.* I stumbled and barely bumped the door. It stopped. The door swung open, and the cold outside air smacked me. *He* stood over me, broom in hand, and glared down at me. *Go back to bed—can't you see I'm dealing with a flood?* I couldn't see anything beyond *his* gargantuan frame. The broom, I could see though. Red droplets splashed the washroom tile.

Twenty years passed, and I forgot. The call came in: *he* died in *his* sleep and the funeral is Wednesday. I drive through the night and cover the distance in a haze. I don't make it in time, but that doesn't matter—to either of *us.* Everyone else pays their respects as I watch from the edge of the cemetery. Before the grave diggers completely cover the casket, I throw in a handful of dirt and the broom.

Sometimes the curtains were blue. They didn't notice though; blindness struck them immune to worldly objects. Their eyes weren't milky, missing, or disconnected. They still saw, but the light couldn't reach their heart anymore.

The curtains shifted colors from blue to deep golden red, mirroring the setting sun.

The house sagged. A depression, an indent, wallowed out in the middle of the parlor. They didn't notice. Pins and needles, static, white noise washed their legs—that buzzing of nerves from sitting too long. And yet, still, they walked. Room to room, pounding along worn carpet paths. Or stumbling after too much afternoon wine.

Noise crashed against the walls. Scratching, vibrating, pillow talk soothed their ears. Voices they thought long gone caressed their memories; music held their rapt attention and commercials played in the distance. Yet they were deaf to the world outside. Misery and loneliness found no place in their home.

The curtains were blue.

Trailer Park Lot #1, Mr. Mays

The last five years have crawled by without you here. Now, I have to start another day, week, year and still no closer to healing our hearts. The kids are angry, and they don't know why; they miss you and don't remember your voice; they love you and can't hug you. Pictures don't hug back, and they don't talk, and they don't give kisses like you. While the day fades blue to pink and finally black, I'm still stuck here—remembering, missing, and not really feeling. It's funny in an angry kind of way how we take people for granted and don't express what they mean to us on a personal level. We always expect them to be there when we wake up, but one day they're just...gone. I read somewhere that our Thakiwaki ways are the hardest because we can't cry. I guess it's true.

A WOLF'S PASSING

The meager lighting comes from the health monitors and the lone ventilator keeping him alive. His labored breathing fills the somber room. Sweat drenches his pale face, leaving a sickly sheen covering him. This man, this weak shriveled man, is not the brother I know, but a ghost inhabiting a desiccated, skinned skeleton.

He was found mowing the same patch of earth—driving in a circle, kicking up dirt clods—slumped over the steering wheel. Instead of calling 911, his neighbor sat him up and gave him a beer. The slurred speech, glazed eyes, and lack of sweating were clues they missed. It was when he couldn't stand that an ambulance was called—after three hours passed.

My phone rings, and an hour later we are driving west. Another hour still and I hear the fear seep through our mother's voice: "It's your brother." I drive. I drive as a man possessed by anger, fear, unknowing, frustration, and the memory of him teaching me how to tie my shoes. Weaving in and out of traffic, shrugging, and talking to myself while my wife sleeps. We make it—not in record time, but still within reason.

Being in public makes no difference; being in the hospital makes no difference either. Whenever my family gathers for any reason, there is always a ruckus. Yelling, shouting, and cursing is the norm. We meet security as we exit the elevator, and I am asked—rudely—what is going on. My mother forces her way between us and the guards: "Not him—the other guy just left."

It is September 2nd.

It's our sister's birthday.

The door opens and closes. My sister appears next to me and studies our brother. To me, he looks like a man running from the devil, but to her, he is just her brother. I know he cannot hear us, but that doesn't stop my sister from asking, "What do you want us to do?" *When it is his time* is the implication of her question, my question. We understand that it will come down to us to make that *decision*—Mom will not, or more to the fact, will be unable to do it.

In this moment, I am suddenly a man. Decisions to be made. Hard decisions. The kind I have no business making and ones I thought he would be making. I never expected to be here. Not now. I look down at his body and reach out to hold his hand. It is clammy cold. All his warmth is gone. It left a long time ago.

Acknowledgments

The following pieces appeared previously:

OSKASHA (OSHKASHÎWIWA)
Schuylkill Valley Journal Online, Dispatches from the Valley, March 2021

INDEPENDENCE DAY
Rejection Letters, August 2020

THE WOLF ARRIVED
Knights Library Literary Magazine, Spring 2020

JACK DANIELS AND A PORCH SWING
Kreaxxion Review, Issue 1 Unsystematic Galore, June 2020

NORTH CULBERHOUSE
Free Flash Fiction, as "407 Kierson Lane" September 24, 2020

2901 PHILADELPHIA COVE
Schuylkill Valley Journal Online, Dispatches from the Valley, July 2020

TRAILER PARK LOT #1, MR MAYS
Mythic Picnic Tweet Story V6, May 2020

Damon McKinney is an Indigenous author currently residing in northeast Arkansas. He has a bachelor of arts degree in English from the University of Arkansas in Little Rock. He's a member of the Sauk and Fox Nation of Oklahoma. His body of work is found on various online literary magazines. He is the former managing editor for *Emerge Literary Journal*, former contributing editor for *Barren Magazine*, and former fiction editor for Likely Red Press. He's been married for twenty-one years to his wife, Sara, and together they have two children.